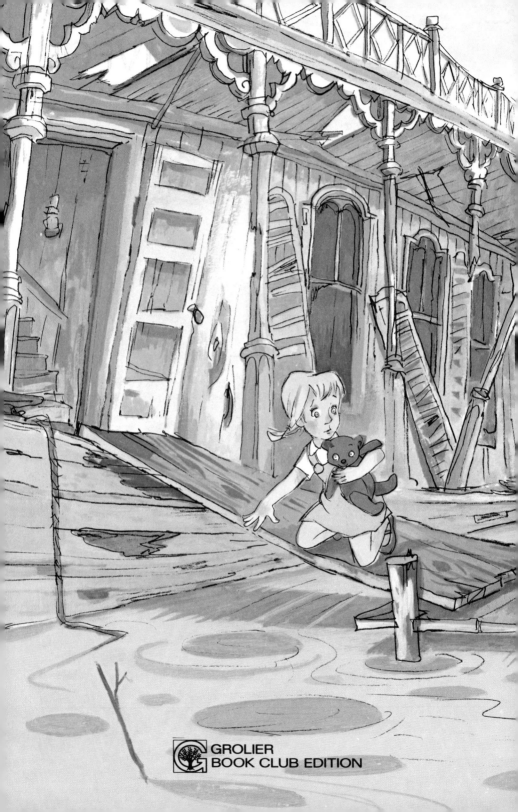

Disney's The Rescuers

Random House  New York

Featuring characters from the Disney film suggested by the books by Margery Sharp, THE RESCUERS and MISS BIANCA, published by Little, Brown and Company.

Library of Congress Cataloging in Publication Data: Main entry under title: The Rescuers. (Disney's wonderful world of reading) Based on a full-length animated film of the same title. Summary: Two enterprising mice rescue a kidnapped orphan. [1. Mice—Fiction. 2. Kidnapping—Fiction] I. Disney (Walt) Productions. PZ7.R313 1977 [E] 76-54412 ISBN 0-394-83456-9 ISBN 0-394-93456-3 lib. bdg.

Manufactured in the United States of America

The Rescue Aid Society was having a meeting.
Mice members had come from all over the world.
"We help anyone . . . anywhere," they all said.

"Someone needs our help now," said Chairman
Mouse. "We found a bottle in the river.
There's a note in it."

Bernard, the janitor, got the note out.

The mice stood around the note. The paper
was wet so the words were hard to read.
But Bianca was a very smart mouse.
She read the note out loud:

Dear Morningside Orphanage,
I am in terrible trouble.
Please hurry.   HELP!
Penny

"Oh, that poor little
girl!" said all the mice.

"Who will go and rescue Penny?"
asked the chairman.

"I will," said Bianca.
"You can't go all by yourself!"
cried the chairman.

Bianca thought a moment. "I'll take Bernard
with me," she said. "We will make a great team."
Bernard was surprised. "Gosh, Miss Bianca!"
he said. "Thanks."

Bernard and Bianca did not
know where Penny was.
But they did know where
Morningside Orphanage was.
They decided to go there.
The night was dark and rainy.
How could they get inside?

MORNINGSIDE
ORPHANAGE

At last they found an open window.
They stood on the window sill and peeked
into the children's room.
All the children were fast asleep.

The rescuers crept inside to have a look
around. Bianca pointed to a closet.

"Let's look in there," she whispered.

Inside the closet the mice saw a big box full of Penny's things. But they did not see Rufus the cat sleeping beside the box.

"Now we're getting somewhere," said Bernard. "At least we know Penny used to live here."

"Shh," said Bianca. "Don't talk so loud!"

Bianca was too late.
All of a sudden Rufus
woke up!
Bernard and Bianca
got ready to run.

"You don't have to worry about me," said
Rufus. "I am too old to chase after mice."
"We are looking for Penny," said Bianca.
"She is in terrible danger."
"Can you tell us where she is?" asked Bernard.

"I am the only one who knows where she is," said Rufus. "But no one has ever asked me."

Rufus told the mice how Penny disappeared. One night a woman named Medusa had come to the orphanage with a man called Snoops. They kidnapped Penny.

"They said they were taking her to look for diamonds in Devil's Bayou," said Rufus.

"Devil's Bayou!" cried Bernard. "How will we ever get there?"

"Don't worry, darling," said Bianca. "We'll fly."

Early the next morning, Bernard and
Bianca rushed to the airport.

Captain Orville of Albatross Airlines
was just coming in for a bumpy landing.

"Flight 13 to Devil's Bayou
takes off in five minutes,"
said the captain.

"Thirteen is not my lucky
number," said Bernard.
"Let's take the train!"
"Nonsense," said Bianca.
"We don't have time."

Bernard and Bianca climbed aboard.
"Fasten your seat belts," said the captain.
Then Captain Orville began to run.

Up . . . up . . .
up they flew.
"I love flying!"
cried Bianca.

Bernard did not love flying. He was scared.
But he soon settled down for the long trip
to Devil's Bayou.

Two days later, Snoops and Medusa were
looking at their stolen jewels on an old boat
in Devil's Bayou.

"We have enough diamonds already, Medusa,"
said Snoops. "Let's get out of this creepy place."

"Are you crazy?" shouted Medusa. "We can't leave until Penny finds the Devil's Eye Diamond. It's the biggest diamond in the world! I want it!"

Snoops and Medusa didn't see Penny tiptoe out the door.

By the time Medusa stopped shouting,
Penny was gone. Medusa was so angry
she gave Snoops a whack on the head.

"I told you to keep your eye on that kid!"
she said. Medusa called to her pet crocodiles:
"Brutus! Nero! Bring Penny back!"

Medusa ran outside and jumped into
her swampmobile. She started the engine
and it began to sputter.

"I will look for Penny myself," said
Medusa as she zoomed away.

Just at that moment, Captain Orville flew over Devil's Bayou. Bernard and Bianca held on tight. The Albatross landed in the swamp with a bump.

The rescuers thanked the captain.
Then they went to meet the swamp folks—
Luke, Ellie Mae, and Evinrude.

"We came here to rescue a girl named Penny,"
said Bianca. "Do you know where she is?"

"She's on the old riverboat," said Ellie Mae.
"But you'll never get her away from Medusa.
Every time the little girl runs off, Medusa
sends those crocodiles after her."

"Here they come now," said Luke.

Bernard and Bianca hid in the grass.
They saw Brutus and Nero carrying Penny
and her teddy bear back to the riverboat.

"We must follow them," said Bianca.

"I can take you," said Evinrude.

Bernard and Bianca got into Evinrude's boat.
Buzz . . . buzz . . . Evinrude flapped his wings.
  "Good luck with the rescue!" called Ellie Mae
as Bernard and Bianca buzzed away.

When the crocodiles brought Penny back to
the boat, Medusa snatched Penny's teddy bear.
"I won't give him back until you find the
Devil's Eye Diamond for me," shouted Medusa.
"I looked all over the cave," said Penny.
"I can't find that diamond anywhere."

"You'll find it tomorrow," said Medusa.
"Or you'll never see your teddy bear again!"

The rescuers waited until Medusa was gone.
Then they jumped onto Penny's window sill.

Penny was very surprised to see the two mice.
"We have come to rescue you," they said.
"Follow us. We'll get away in the swampmobile."
But Penny didn't want to go without her teddy
bear. So Bernard and Bianca hid in her room.
"We'll help you find the diamond," they said.

The next morning Medusa and Snoops led Penny into the swamp. They took her to the Black Hole to look for the Devil's Eye Diamond.

Penny held on to a long rope, and Snoops and Medusa dropped her into the deep hole. But Penny was not afraid. Bernard and Bianca were hiding in her pocket.

When they reached the bottom, Penny shined her light all around. "This was a pirates' cave," she said. "It's full of diamonds. But Medusa wants the big one."

"Well, let's look for it," said Bianca. "Then we can get your teddy bear and go home."

Suddenly Bernard ran into a corner.
He saw some old pirate's bones.
And he saw something big and shiny.
"I think I found it!" cried Bernard.

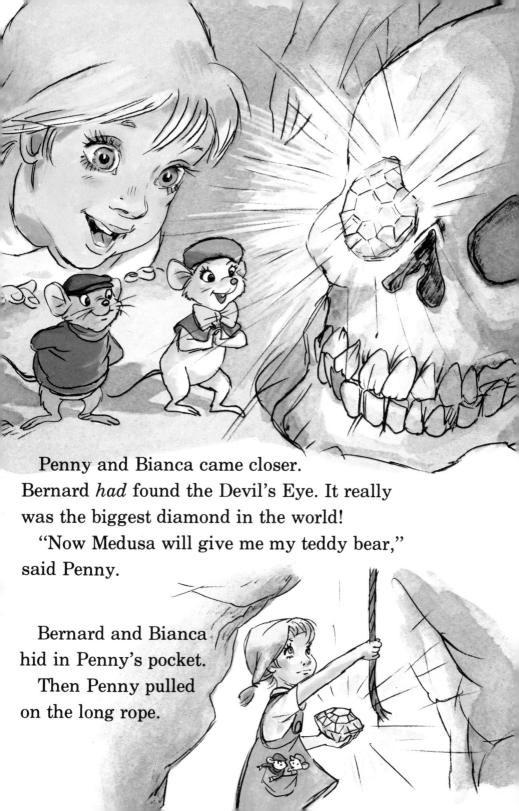

Penny and Bianca came closer.
Bernard *had* found the Devil's Eye. It really
was the biggest diamond in the world!
"Now Medusa will give me my teddy bear,"
said Penny.

Bernard and Bianca
hid in Penny's pocket.
Then Penny pulled
on the long rope.

Snoops pulled Penny up quickly.
As soon as Medusa saw
the Devil's Eye, she grabbed it.

"Oh, my beautiful diamond,"
she said.
"*Your* diamond!"
Snoops cried.
"Half of that diamond
is mine!" He tried
to look at it.

Medusa gave Snoops a hard push.

"Get away from me, Fatso!" she shouted.
"I am taking the diamond, and
the teddy bear, too."

Medusa started running
toward the boat.

The others followed her
as fast as they could go.

Medusa rushed into her room and
took out a needle and thread. She began
to sew the diamond into Penny's teddy bear.

"I will leave Snoops and Penny here
in Devil's Bayou," said Medusa.
"The diamond will be all mine!"

Just as Medusa had finished sewing,
Snoops burst through the door.

"Give me my half of that diamond!" he said.

Penny was right behind him.

"Give me my teddy bear!" she said.

Medusa put the teddy
bear under her arm
and began to run.

But Medusa did not look where she was going.
Suddenly she tripped on a loose floor board.
   Up into the air went the teddy bear!
   Down onto the floor went Medusa!

Penny reached out to catch
her teddy bear.

"Run for the swampmobile!"
cried Bernard and Bianca.

Holding on to her teddy bear,
Penny ran to the swampmobile.
One . . . two . . . three . . .
Bernard and Bianca and Penny
all jumped in.

Then Penny tried to start the engine.
The swampmobile began to sputter.
It started! Penny zoomed away.

"Hooray! Hooray!" cried Bernard and
Bianca, dancing on the steering wheel.

"Stop! Stop!" shouted Snoops.
"Bring back my diamond!" cried Medusa.
But Penny and the rescuers did not hear
them. They were on their way home.

Two days later the Rescue Aid Society had
another meeting. The mice were watching
Penny on the news. She told the man how
she had found the diamond in her teddy bear.
Now it belonged to Morningside Orphanage.

"But how did you get away?" asked the man.

"Two little mice rescued me," said Penny.

"Three cheers for Bernard and Bianca!"
cried all the mice.

When the meeting was over,
the chairman read a note.
Someone else was in trouble.

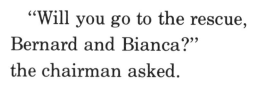

"Will you go to the rescue,
Bernard and Bianca?"
the chairman asked.

"Shall we go?" said Bianca.
"Of course," said Bernard.
"We make a great team."

Once again, Bernard and Bianca flew up
into the air with Captain Orville.
The rescuers were off on another long trip.
"We help anyone . . . anywhere!" they said.